© 1995 Twin Books Ltd

Produced by
TWIN BOOKS
Kimbolton House
117a Fulham Road
London SW3 6RL

Directed by CND – Muriel Nathan-Deiller
Illustrated by Van Gool-Lefèvre-Loiseaux

ISBN: 1 85469 063 9

Printed in China

Beauty and the Beast

Van Gool

TWIN BOOKS

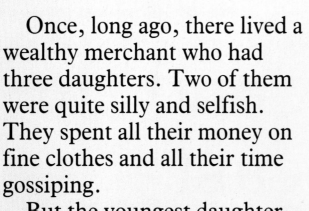

Once, long ago, there lived a wealthy merchant who had three daughters. Two of them were quite silly and selfish. They spent all their money on fine clothes and all their time gossiping.

But the youngest daughter, who was called Beauty because she was so fair, had a kind and generous nature. She saw only the good in everyone.

One day, Beauty and her sisters overheard some very bad news through the open windows. All their father's ships had been lost at sea—and with them, all their money.

Beauty's sisters made such a fuss at the idea of being poor that their father was very unhappy. He went to his bankers to borrow money, but they refused him.

The merchant went home and told his daughters, "There is only one hope of regaining our fortune. I heard today that one of my ships may have landed safely with a rich cargo. I must go to a distant port and find out if this is true."

Eagerly, his older daughters cried, "What wonderful news, Father! If the ship has come in, please bring back some new silk gowns and beautiful jewels."

"And you, Beauty?" asked her father.

"Only come back safely, and bring me a single rose to brighten the winter," she replied.

After a long, cold journey, the merchant found that his last ship had indeed come into port. He sold its cargo for a goodly sum, but on his way home he became lost in the forest.

Suddenly, a tiny purple elf appeared in the air before him. "Follow me," said the elf. And he led the merchant to the gateway of a huge palace.

As he passed through the gateway, the tired traveler was astonished to see that he had left winter behind. The walls of the palace melted away, and he found himself in a spacious hall warmed by a big fire. The elf led him through one beautiful room after another. But there was no one to be seen.

Finally, the merchant came to a banquet hall, where the table was set with the finest foods. He was very hungry, so he helped himself to the feast and fell asleep before the fire.

In the morning, the merchant tried to find the owner of the palace to thank him for his hospitality. But still he found no one. As he was leaving, he stopped in the courtyard to pick a rose for Beauty.

Suddenly, a fierce voice roared behind him, and he turned to see a frightful Beast.

"So this is how you repay my kindness—by stealing my flowers! You shall die for this!" said the Beast.

The terrified merchant fell down before the Beast and told him the story of his journey and of his promise to Beauty.

"See if she loves you enough to save your life," growled the Beast. "Let her come here of her own free will one month from today, or I will come and find you."

The poor merchant turned homeward at a very slow pace. He knew he could not hand Beauty over to the Beast.

When his older daughters came out to greet him, they were thrilled with the lavish gifts he had brought them. But when he handed Beauty her rose, he said sadly, "Little do you know what it cost." Then he told her of the Beast's command.

Hiding her terror, Beauty said calmly, "Of course, I will go, Father. The Beast will not harm me. Perhaps he's lonely in that great palace. But you must stay here and look after your business. I'll soon be home for a visit."

Her father's faithful horse carried Beauty safely to the palace of the Beast.

21

Beauty hesitated when she reached the great courtyard, but the purple elf appeared to guide her.

"This way!" he cried, and Beauty followed him into the palace, still trembling for fear of the Beast.

The elf led Beauty to a handsome bedroom filled with fine furniture. Satin hangings tied with gold cords draped the windows. On the dressing table was a jewelry box filled with priceless gems and a dozen of the roses Beauty loved.

"All these are yours," said the eif. "Gifts from my master."

Then Beauty noticed a huge wardrobe chest filled with silk and velvet gowns, beaded slippers and colorful headdresses.

Beauty took off her simple traveling clothes and tried on one of the elegant gowns from the wardrobe. When she looked into the mirror, she scarcely knew herself, so grown-up and lovely did she look.

"Truly, you deserve your name," said the elf admiringly.

Beauty had almost forgotten her fear of the Beast—until suddenly, he appeared at her side. When she saw how huge and ugly he was, she shrank away and stifled a scream. But he looked so unhappy when he saw her distress that she calmed herself at once.

"Good evening, Beast," she said with a curtsy.

"It is good to have you here, Beauty," he replied. "I hope we can spend some time together every evening and get to know one another. It has been very lonely here for many a year."

"I look forward to it," said Beauty warmly. And so they began to meet and talk together daily. Soon Beauty looked forward to the Beast's visits, as she had no other companion than the friendly elf.

Each night, the Beast led Beauty to the banquet hall, where the table was set with all kinds of delicacies. The Beast ate nothing, but Beauty had her dinner at the fireside while they talked.

One night, as the clock chimed nine, the Beast beckoned Beauty onto the terrace. There he asked, "Did you truly come here of your own free will?"

"Yes," said Beauty. "Your kindness in sparing my father's life made me eager to keep his promise to you. And your kindness to me has made me feel very welcome."

"Then you shall come and go freely, as you wish," said the Beast. "But first, I must ask you: could you learn to love me?"

Beauty's heart sank, but she answered honestly, "I hope that I can."

"Very well then," said the Beast, turning away. "You may go home for awhile. But I trust you to come back in a month's time."

Beauty's father was overjoyed when she returned. In his heart, he had feared he would never see her again.

"The Beast was very kind to me" Beauty assured him. "And I have promised to go back to him." She dared not tell her father that the Beast wished to marry her. The idea was too new—and too frightening.

Weeks passed away, and Beauty keep putting off her return to the Beast's palace. But one night, her elf friend appeared to her in a dream. She saw the Beast with bowed head at his gateway, watching out for her return, but losing hope. Dead leaves blew around him, and he sighed deeply.

In the morning, Beauty told her sisters that she must return at once to the Beast's palace.

"What are you thinking of?" they cried. "Do you mean to leave your family forever? Stay here where you are safe, and never think of that dreadful Beast again."

But Beauty would not be persuaded. "I promised to go back, and I must," she said. "He misses me very much. I dreamed that he was growing lonelier and weaker every day."

Putting on one of the beautiful gowns the Beast had given her, Beauty took the forest path to the palace. From a distance, it looked dark and deserted.

Frightened, Beauty followed the elf into the courtyard. There, as in her dream, the dry leaves swirled. But the reality was even worse than the dream. The Beast lay on the broken pavement at the point of death.

"Forgive me!" cried Beauty. "I have come back to stay as long as you wish."

"Can you really love such an ugly creature as I am?" asked the Beast faintly.

"Yes," answered Beauty. "No one could call you ugly who really knew you, as I do."

With that, a blaze of light filled the courtyard, and the Beast was transformed before Beauty's eyes into a handsome prince.

"Your love has broken the evil spell that held me prisoner as a Beast," said the prince. "Will you be my wife?"

"I will," said Beauty.

"Here is our home," said the prince, as a palace more splendid than before rose from the clouds.

The happy couple sent for Beauty's family to attend their wedding. The prince's family, too, arrived, to celebrate his release from his long loneliness.

Thus, Beauty and the prince were married, to general rejoicing, and lived to enjoy many years of happiness and peace together.